Little Quack's Hide AND Seek

by **Lauren Thompson**

pictures by **Derek Anderson**

SCHOLASTIC INC.

New York Toronto London Auckland Sydney
Mexico City New Delhi Hong Kong Buenos Aires

Mama Duck had five little ducklings, Widdle, Waddle, Piddle, Puddle, and Little Quack.

One day Mama said, "Let's play hide-and-seek. You hide, and I'll try to find you."

COUNT ALONG WITH THE QUACK–U–LATOR!

🐥 🐥 🐥 🐥 🐥 = 5

"You won't find *me*!" cried Widdle.
"You'll never find *me*!" cried Waddle.
"Just try and find *me*!" cried Piddle.
"You'll find me *last*!" cried Puddle.
And Little Quack cried, "I'll find the *BEST* hiding place of all!"

FIVE DUCKLINGS

Mama covered her eyes. She began to count, "One . . . two . . ."
Widdle found a dark place to hide.

FOUR DUCKLINGS

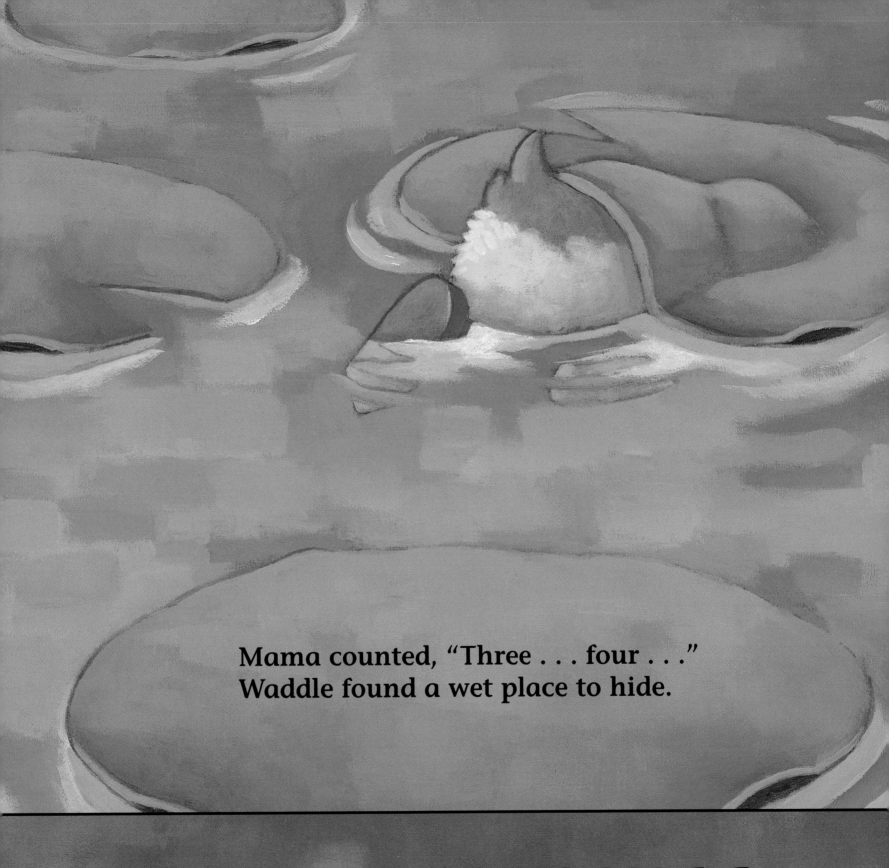

Mama counted, "Three . . . four . . ."
Waddle found a wet place to hide.

THREE DUCKLINGS

Mama counted, "Five . . . six . . ."
Piddle found a high place to hide.

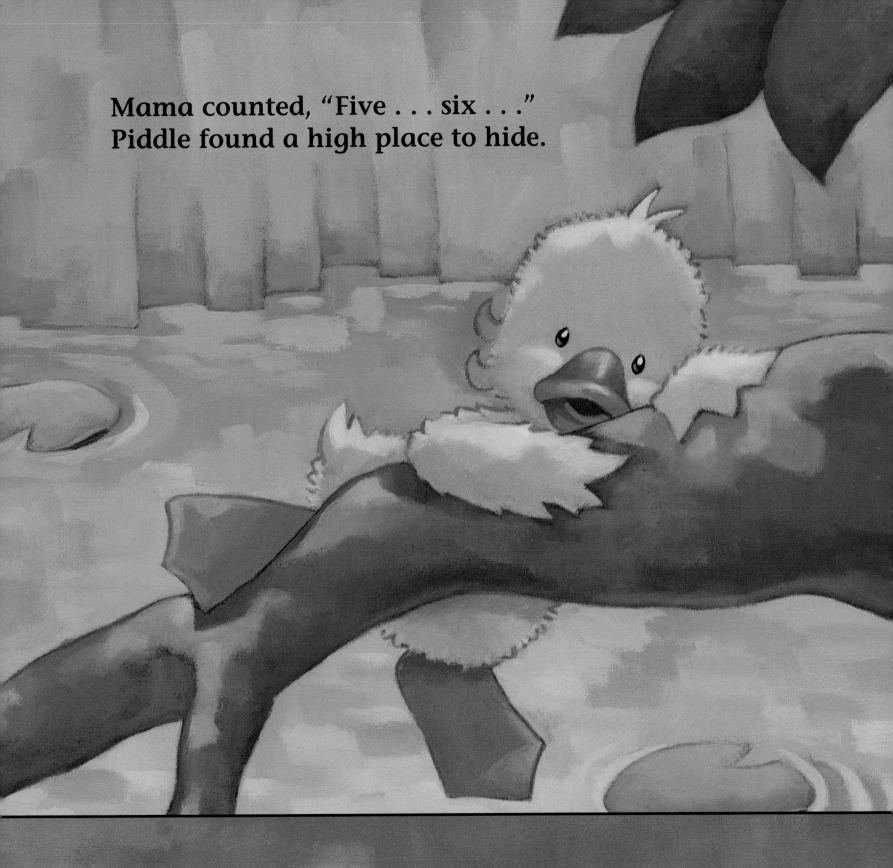

TWO DUCKLINGS

Mama Duck counted, "Seven . . . eight . . ."
Puddle found a leafy place to hide.

ONE DUCKLING

Mama counted, "Nine . . ."
Oh, no! Where should Little Quack hide?

Mama called out, "Ten! Here I come!"
Little Quack found a *quick* place to hide
—right behind Mama!

Mama paddled over to a log.
"Any ducklings down there?" she called.
"Here I am!" cried Widdle.
"That's one little duckling found," said Mama.
"Who will I find next?"

Mama paddled over to the lilies.
"Any ducklings under here?" she called.
"You found me!" cried Waddle.
"That's two little ducklings found," said Mama.
"Who will I find next?"

Mama paddled over to a branch.
"Any ducklings up there?" she called.
"It's me!" cried Piddle.
"That's three little ducklings found," said Mama.
"Who will I find next?"

Mama paddled over to the reeds.
"Any ducklings here?" she called.
"I'm here!" called Puddle.
"That's four little ducklings found," said
Mama. "Now, where is Little Quack?"

Mama paddled over to the shore.
"Little Quack, are you hiding here?" she called.
No, Little Quack wasn't hiding on the shore.

Mama paddled over to a rock.
"Little Quack, are you are hiding here?" she called.
No, Little Quack wasn't hiding near the rock.

Then Mama Duck called out,
"Little Quack, where *are* you?"

"Here I am!" cried Little Quack. "Right behind you, Mama!"
"There you are!" said Mama. "You *did* find the best hiding place of all!"

Then, *quack, quack quack!* laughed Mama with her ducklings, Widdle, Waddle, Piddle, Puddle—and the *quackiest* of all was Little Quack.

**To Owen, our "quacky"
little duckling
—L. T.**

**For Mom and Dad
—D. A.**

ISBN 0-439-76104-2

12 11 10 9 8 7 6 5 4 3   8 9 10/0

Printed in the U.S.A.   08

First Scholastic printing, March 2005

Book design by Greg Stadnyk
The text for this book is set in Stone Informal and 99.
The illustrations for this book are rendered in acrylic on canvas.